HICKORY STICK RAG

By Clyde and Wendy Watson:

FATHER FOX'S PENNYRHYMES
TOM FOX AND THE APPLE PIE
QUIPS & QUIRKS
HICKORY STICK RAG

Hickory Stick Rag

BY CLYDE WATSON

ILLUSTRATED BY WENDY WATSON

Thomas Y. Crowell Company, New York

Library of Congress Cataloging in Publication Data

Watson, Clyde. Hickory stick rag.

SUMMARY: Recounts in rhyme the good and bad events
of the school year.   [1. School stories. 2. Stories in rhyme]
I. Watson, Wendy. II. Title. PZ8.3.W28Hi   [E]   75-6607
ISBN 0-690-00959-3 ISBN 0-690-00960-7 (lib. bdg.)

1   2   3   4   5   6   7   8   9   10

Hickory Stick Rag

Cross as two sticks
And thin as a bean,
We once had a schoolteacher
Cranky & mean.

We ran up the steps
On our very first day,
We skipped & whistled
And sang the whole way.

She stood there to greet us
So nasty & sour
We shook in our shoes
For the next half an hour..

"Now children!" she cackled,
"Begin Lesson One!
I'll have no more noise
For school has begun!"

We didn't dare talk
And we didn't dare laugh
And if we passed notes
She just ripped them in half.

She made us add numbers,
She made us spell words,
There must be more to it
Or school's for the birds.

Day in & day out
From nine until three
We sat there, bored stiff
'Til the bell set us free.

On Monday we sighed,
On Tuesday we cursed,
But Wednesday & Thursday
And Friday were worse.

By the end of the week
It became pretty clear
What a mess we were in
For the rest of the year.

"How can we stand it?"
We asked with a hiss,
"One hundred & seventy
More days like this?!"

Like it or lump it,
What else could we do
But liven things up
With a neat trick or two?

Spitballs & stinkbombs
On hot afternoons,
Peashooters, squirtguns
And water balloons.

Bad words on the blackboard
And tacks on her chair,
Mysterious noises
And smoke in the air.

Strange flying objects
Of all shapes & sizes,
Booby traps, bees' nests
And other surprises.

Whenever she caught us
She gave us the dickens,
We all had our share
Of her lectures & lickings.

Piffle & poppycock
That's how it goes,
How we put up with it
Nobody knows.

Once in a while
Without any warning
School was called off
First thing in the morning.

We'd all be snowed in
By a fabulous blizzard
Or she would stay home
With a cold in her gizzard.

The plumbing would freeze
Or the stove wouldn't heat
Or the bus wouldn't run
On account of the sleet.

In spite of our hopes
Such occasions were rare
So we took our own holidays,
That's only fair.

Some kids played hooky,
Quite risky, but fun,
And some had excuses
While others had none.

Every so often
Somebody got sick:
Bellyache, sniffles
Or chills did the trick.

The rest of the time
We were stuck there in class
So we figured out ways
To make the time pass.

Cartoons & comic strips,
How did you guess?
Chocolates & chiclets
And checkers & chess.

Secrets in code
And invisible inks,
Puzzles & poker
And tiddlywinks.

Slowly we crossed off
The weeks of the year
When all of a sudden
Sweet summer was near.

The sky was bright blue,
We could hardly sit still
For dreaming of strawberries
Out on the hill.

At last, at long last
Our wishes came true:
She dismissed us for good
And school was all through.

But that isn't all—
We had one more surprise:
And this time we asked her
To cover her eyes.

With fanfare & flags
She was marched out the door
And we gave her a party
With good things galore.

A fancy round cake
With roses on top,
Confetti & pinwheels
And cold ginger pop.

Then leaping & laughing
We hurried away
Shouting "NO MORE SCHOOL!
HIP HIP HOORAY!"

125504

Clyde and Wendy Watson

are sisters. They grew up in a large, lively, and creative family, nearly every member of which is a writer or an artist. Clyde is a graduate of Smith College and has taught in several schools, including one on an Indian reservation. She is an accomplished musician and composer, as well as a writer. Wendy, a graduate of Bryn Mawr College, has illustrated more than thirty books and has won many prizes and awards for her distinguished artwork. She is married and is the mother of a small child.

Besides HICKORY STICK RAG, they have collaborated on several other books, including *Quips and Quirks, Tom Fox and the Apple Pie* and *Father Fox's Penny-rhymes*. The latter was designated a Notable Book by the American Library Association, was runner-up for the National Book Award in 1972, and has established itself firmly as a modern American classic.